Clifford THE BIG RED DOG®

THE SNOW DOG

By Lisa Ann Marsoli
Illustrated by Steve Haefele

D0033297

Based on the Scholastic book series "Clifford The Big Red Dog" by Norman Bridwell

10 9 8 7 6 5 4 3 2 1   04 05 06 07 08

Printed in the U.S.A.
First printing, January 2004

SCHOLASTIC INC.

New York   Toronto   London   Auckland   Sydney
Mexico City   New Delhi   Hong Kong   Buenos Aires

"Clifford, look!" said Emily Elizabeth.

It had been snowing all night.

The yard was covered with snow.

Emily Elizabeth put a big scarf on Clifford.

They were ready to play!

Clifford made a snowball.

He rolled it with his nose.

Clifford rolled the snowball across the yard.

He rolled it down the street.

"Clifford, where are you going?"

called Emily Elizabeth.

A few minutes later, she got a big surprise.

It was a giant runaway snowball!

"Oh, Clifford! It's you!"

Emily Elizabeth said.

She watched as Clifford built

a supersize frozen snack.

Soon the yard was full of snow art.

Charley, Jetta, and Vaz came by.

"Wow!" said Charley. "Those look terrific!"

"There's a snow sculpture contest tomorrow,"

Jetta told them. "You and Clifford should enter."

"That's a great idea!" said Emily Elizabeth.

Clifford wagged his tail.

Then they headed off for some more winter fun.

They went "dogsledding."

They ice-skated.

And they built a towering snow fort.

Clifford was the lookout.

The next day, Emily Elizabeth and Clifford

set off for the snow sculpture contest.

They stopped to catch snowflakes.

"Come on," said Emily Elizabeth,

"we're going to be late."

They ran the rest of the way to the park.

Then Emily Elizabeth went to sign them up.

Clifford lay down and quickly fell asleep.

All that running had worn him out!

Emily Elizabeth came back.

She looked around.

Where could Clifford be?

"He's probably making a big snowball

somewhere," Emily Elizabeth decided.

Emily Elizabeth spotted the pile

of snow next to her.

She got right to work smoothing

and patting it into shape.

Thirty minutes passed.

The contest was almost over.

"Has anyone seen Clifford?"

Emily Elizabeth asked.

"No," said Charley.

"But I see the judges."

They admired Emily Elizabeth's snow dog.

"It looks so real!" said Mr. Kibble.

"In fact, it looks a lot like Clifford."

"Where is Clifford?" wondered Mrs. Diller.

Suddenly, Emily Elizabeth's

snow sculpture burst open.

What a surprise! Clifford was inside!

The delicious smells from the table had

woken him up.

The judges gave out the awards. Jetta's snow castle won a ribbon for the prettiest snow sculpture.

Charlie's snow skateboard won the
"Most Original" award.

Vaz's snowman was the silliest.

And Clifford ate some treats.

The judges made up a new award just

for Emily Elizabeth and Clifford. . . .

"Hungriest"!

The big red snow dog wore it proudly.

Do You Remember?

Circle the right answer.

1. What did Clifford use his giant snowball to build?

    a. A doghouse
    b. A bone
    c. A dog

2. Why did Clifford fall asleep?
    a. He was tired from the day before.
    b. He got up too early.
    c. He ran all the way to the park.

Which happened first?
Which happened next?
Which happened last?

Write a 1, 2, or 3 in the space after each sentence.

The park worker blew snow onto Clifford. _____

Emily Elizabeth and her friends went sledding. _____

Jetta won the prize for the prettiest snow sculpture. _____

Answers:

Jetta won the prize for the prettiest snow sculpture. (3)
Emily Elizabeth and her friends went sledding. (1)
The park worker blew snow onto Clifford. (2)
2. c
1. b